DOG LOVES COUNTING

LOUISE YATES

RED FOX

For Owen

Some other books by Louise Yates

A Small Surprise

Dog Loves Books

Dog Loves Drawing

Frank & Teddy Make Friends

DOG LOVES COUNTING
A RED FOX BOOK 978 1 849 41548 4

First published in Great Britain by Jonathan Cape,
an imprint of Random House Children's Publishers UK
A Random House Group Company

Jonathan Cape edition published 2013
Red Fox edition published 2013

1 3 5 7 9 10 8 6 4 2

Copyright © Louise Yates, 2013

The right of Louise Yates to be identified as the author and illustrator of this work has
been asserted in accordance with the Copyright, Designs and Patents Act 1988.

Red Fox Books are published by Random House Children's Publishers UK,
61–63 Uxbridge Road, London W5 5SA

www.**randomhousechildrens**.co.uk
www.**randomhouse**.co.uk

Addresses for companies within The Random House Group Limited can be found at: www.randomhouse.co.uk/offices.htm

THE RANDOM HOUSE GROUP Limited Reg. No. 954009

A CIP catalogue record for this book is available from the British Library.

Printed in China

The Random House Group Limited supports the Forest Stewardship Council® (FSC®), the leading international forest-certification organisation.
Our books carrying the FSC label are printed on FSC®-certified paper. FSC is the only forest-certification scheme supported by the leading
environmental organisations, including Greenpeace. Our paper procurement policy can be found at www.randomhouse.co.uk/environment

FSC
www.fsc.org

MIX
Paper from
responsible sources
FSC® C020056

Dog loved books. He loved reading
them late into the night and didn't like
to leave them for long.

He knew he must
sleep, but Dog
just couldn't drift
off. He tried
counting sheep,
but they weren't
helping at all.

"Perhaps there are other creatures
I could count?" he thought.

Dog reached for a book and began.

The first thing Dog found was an egg.

"One," he counted, and the egg began to hatch.

Inside was a baby dodo.
"Hello, little one," said Dog.
He looked around, but
the dodo was
all alone.

N°2
Dog

N°1
The Dodo

"I'll look after you," said Dog. "Together
we are two. Number One, follow me –
we must find Number Three."

They looked on through the book for
the next creature they could count.
"Number Three?" Dog called out.

"Are you speaking to
me?" said a sloth
after a long silence.
He waved very, very slowly.

1 2 3

N.º3
The
Three-Toed
Sloth

Dog counted his claws.

The three-toed sloth wanted to help them find more numbers. He took his time, but together they continued on, keeping count all the way.

1... 2...3...

"Four!" cried a camel. "One, two, three, four!"
He counted out on his legs.

"We are counting," explained Dog,
"so that I can fall asleep."

The camel hoped he could help. "In the desert where I come from, there are many more things we can count. Follow me!"

Nº4
The Camel

1

2   3   4

"The next number is five," said the camel. "There is a lizard, I think, called a five-lined skink."

They found him under a log.

"Hello," said the skink.
"May we count your
lines?" asked Dog.
"Of course," said
the skink.

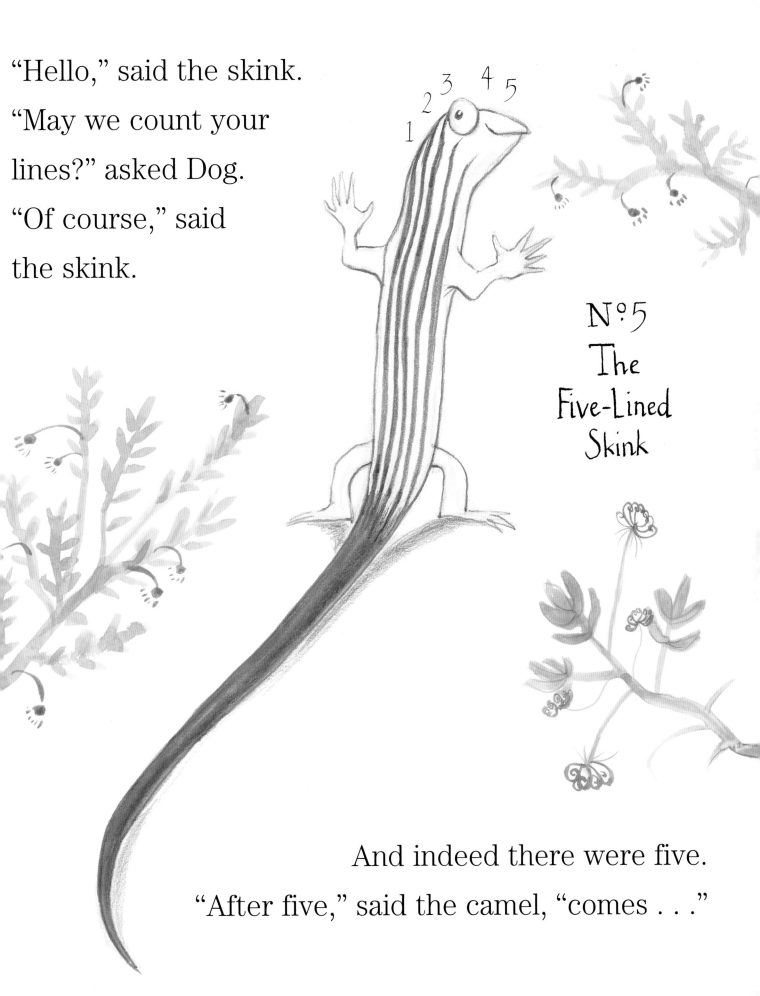

N°5
The
Five-Lined
Skink

And indeed there were five.
"After five," said the camel, "comes . . ."

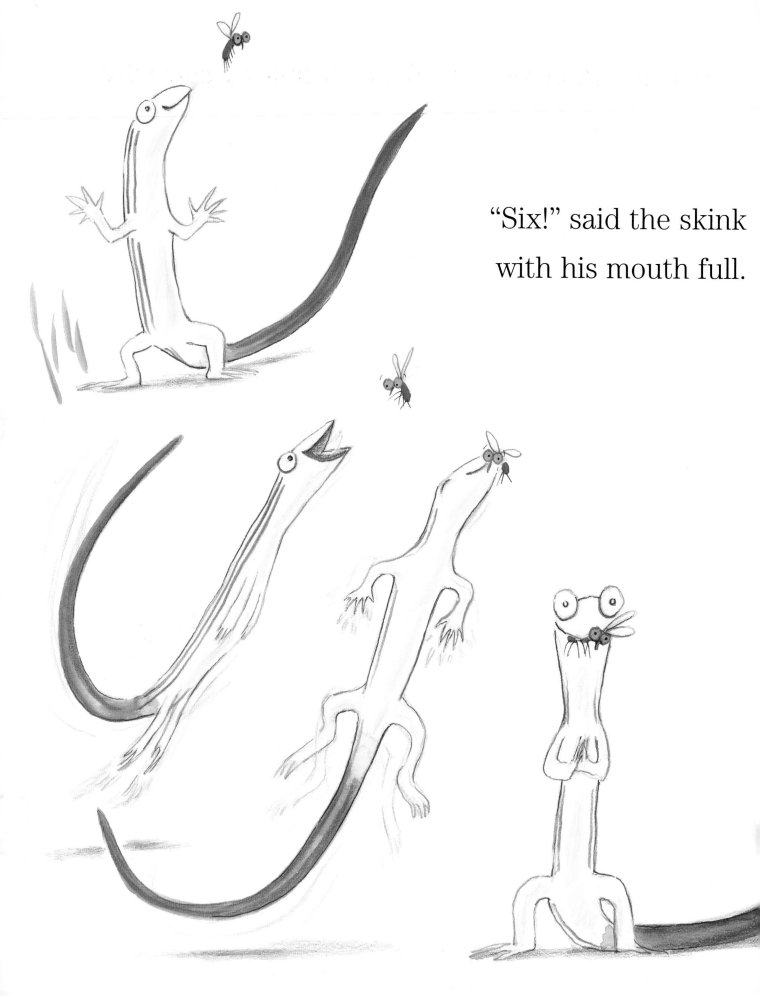

"Six!" said the skink
with his mouth full.

And as he untangled the fly, they quickly saw why.

1 2 3 4 5 6

Nº6
The Fly

"Coooo-eeee!" called a . . .

. . . raccoon, waving her tail.

She had seven black stripes.

Nº7
The Raccoon

1 2

3

4

5   6   7

"We're on our way to the desert," said Dog.

"Can I come too?" called a spider. "Or am I too late?"

1   2   3   4   5   6   7   8

Nº8
The Spider

"Just in time," replied Dog, and they counted to eight.

Number Nine was harder to find –

he was dozing in his burrow.

"Who's in there?" called Dog.

"A nine-banded armadillo," said a voice.

123456789

And when the creature came out, they saw it was true.

He joined them too.

"Nearly there," said the camel.

"What number's next?" asked the armadillo.

"Ten!" called a crab, and he scuttled about waving each leg in turn.

Nº10
The Crab

Dog was enjoying himself!
He couldn't wait to know
more numbers.

But when at last they did reach the desert, Dog was disappointed. There was nothing to count as far as he could see.

"Don't worry," said the camel. "There are as many numbers here as there are grains of sand beneath our feet."

"Let's all count together," said Dog cheerfully.
"Number One . . ." he began.

But Number One was nowhere to be seen!

"We've lost One!"
cried Dog.
"We must find him!"

They were all
very worried.

So they split up and set off, searching in different directions.

There were ten, 10

then nine, 9

then eight, 8

then seven, 7

then six, 6

then five,

5

then four,

4

then three,

3

then two,

2

and then . . .

. . . there was # One.

He was looking up at the stars.
They all joined him, counting up and up,
higher and higher and higher.

Dog loves counting!

"I could do this for ever," he said
happily. The others agreed.

When Dog woke up the next morning and looked
at his books, he knew that friends and adventures
were never far away – that was something
he could count on.